DOG'S
COLORFUL DAY

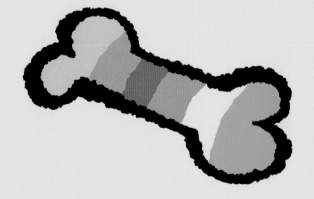

PUFFIN BOOKS
Published by the Penguin Group
Penguin Putnam Books for Young Readers,
345 Hudson Street, New York, New York 10014, U.S.A.
Penguin Books Ltd, 80 Strand, London WC2R ORL, England
Penguin Books Australia Ltd, Ringwood, Victoria, Australia
Penguin Books Canada Ltd, 10 Alcorn Avenue, Toronto, Ontario, Canada M4V 3B2
Penguin Books (N.Z.) Ltd, 182-190 Wairau Road, Auckland 10, New Zealand

Penguin Books Ltd, Registered Offices: Harmondsworth, Middlesex, England

First published in the United States of America by Dutton Children's Books,
a division of Penguin Putnam Books for Young Readers, 2001
Published by Puffin Books, a division of
Penguin Putnam Books for Young Readers, 2003

32 33 34 35 36 37 38 39 40

Copyright © Tucker Slingsby Ltd, 2000
All rights reserved

CIP data is available.

Puffin Books ISBN 978-0-14-250019-4

Manufactured in China

Dog's COLORFUL DAY

A MeSSy Story about Colors and Counting

Emma Dodd

PUFFIN BOOKS

This is Dog.

As you can see, Dog is white with one black spot on his left ear.

At breakfast time,
Dog sits under
the table, as usual.

Splat!

A drip of red jam
lands on his back.

Now Dog has
two spots.

After breakfast, Dog runs outside.

He slips past the man
painting the front door.

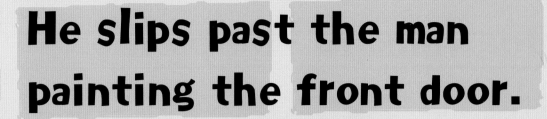

Splish!

His tail dips into
the blue paint.

Now Dog has three spots.

Dog runs to the park
and rolls on the grass.

Squash!

The grass makes a green
stain on his white coat.

Now Dog has four spots.

Dog follows a little boy
eating chocolate.

Squish!

The boy gives Dog a
chocolaty pat—
but no chocolate.

Now Dog has
five spots.

A bee buzzes up to
see what is going on.

Swish!

The bee drops yellow
pollen as it flies by.

Now Dog has six spots.

Dog trots on
through the park.

Splosh!

A drop of pink
ice cream lands
on his right ear.

Now Dog has
seven spots.

Time to go home.
Dog runs up the street.

Splash!

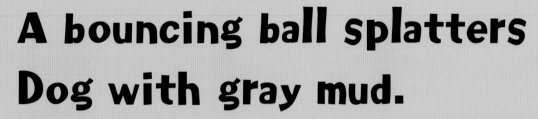

**A bouncing ball splatters
Dog with gray mud.**

Now Dog has eight spots.

In front of the gate,
Dog steps on a carton
of orange juice.

Splurt!

A patch of orange
appears on his leg.

Now Dog has nine spots.

Dog races back inside the house and knocks right into Vicky.

"Silly Dog!"

Vicky's purple marker leaves a smudge on Dog's head.

Now Dog has ten spots.

Vicky looks down at Dog.
She counts his colorful spots.

1 2 3 4 5

6 7 8 9 10!

**Vicky looks more closely.
Dog has...**

a red spot
of jam,

a blue blob
of paint,

a green stain
of grass,

a yellow
patch
of pollen,

a brown
smear of
chocolate,

a pink **drop** of ice cream,

a gray **splatter** of mud,

an orange **splash** of juice,

a purple **smudge** of ink,

and, of course, a black **spot** on his left ear!

"You need a bath, Dog!"

When Dog climbs into bed, he has just one black spot on his left ear.

Good night, Dog.

What a colorful day you've had!

MAR 2019 (2001)